FORESHORE
Classic Short Fiction

ABOUT THE AUTHOR

Paul `Pops` Westlake was born and raised in Plymouth, Devon where he still lives today. He served in the Royal Navy for 11 years, and has worked as a road sweeper, bookmaker, and security guard. *The Boss* is his debut novella. His previous work includes *By Pure Chance* and *The Walters Boys.*

PAUL WESTLAKE

THE BOSS

FORESHORE PUBLISHING
London

Published by Foreshore Publishing 2022.
The home of quality short fiction.

Copyright © Paul Westlake 2022

The Forge 397-411 Westferry Road,
Isle of Dogs, London, E14 3AE

Foreshore Publishing Limited Reg. No. 13358650

ISBN 978-1-9168790-6-5

www.foreshorepublishing.com

Cover design by Andjela Vujic

CONTENTS

PART ONE

The Start

Everywhere was calm, peaceful, and nothing at all exciting appeared to be happening. In fact, many might say that it all looked rather boring on this particular evening in 1998. As dull and lifeless as it undoubtedly was, it suited Jack right down to the ground, especially after a long and tiring week at work.

He also couldn't care less that, whilst he sat in his favourite armchair, he looked much older than he really was, and if he had a pipe and slippers on now, it would have suited him perfectly. He just wanted some peace and quiet to read his newspaper.

"Oh my God, yes! Now we're talking!" he exclaimed, excitedly, shattering the peace and serenity. "A Tarantino classic!"

Rather conveniently, the television remote control just happened to be nestling on the arm right next to him. He was in so much of a rush to pick it up, he nearly dropped on the floor before pointing it straight at the television and then click as he waited and waited, but the screen remained black. He tried again, but it was the same result.

"Bloody hell, what's wrong with this thing?" he said, before making two more attempts, but the screen remained black.

"Batteries must have run out," he said to himself before huffing and puffing his way over to the television to see if he could find out how to turn it on manually.

Before he did that, he checked that it was plugged in and switched on, which it was, checked all the leads were connected, which they appeared to be, so, it was just a matter of trying to figure out the switches that ran down the side of the set.

Easier said than done. Because at first glance, they may just as well have been a set of Egyptian hieroglyphics for all the sense that they made to him.

The film was starting soon, and he had to decide, so he chose the one coloured in green in the hope that it would be the one. Sadly, it wasn't, and the screen just stayed black. In frustration, he tried every single switch, but to no avail, and not being able to think of anything else to do, he slumped disappointedly back in his armchair.

"I don't believe it," he said. "An absolute master-piece of filmmaking and the telly refuses to work. And it's supposed to be brand new as well."

He gave a huge, disappointed sigh. All he could do for now was go back to his newspaper, but obviously turning over from the TV guide, as there was no need to be reading that anymore, at least for now.

"Hello Jack."

There was no need for Jack to turn around; he clearly recognised the young woman's voice. It belonged to his flat mate and lifelong friend Mandy.

"Oh hello, didn`t know that you were home," Jack said.

"Yeah, came home a few hours ago and went straight to my room for a sleep. Was feeling shattered," Mandy said, rubbing the sleep from her eyes.

"Oh right, anyway, glad you're home, got something to ask you," Jack said.

"Yeah, what's that then?"

"Where did you get this TV from?" "Why?"

"Because it doesn't work, that's why, and there's a Tarantino classic due to start anytime now and I'm going to miss it."

"Oh right," she answered, not seemingly particularly bothered about his plight.

"So, where was it from then? Curry's, Dixons, somewhere like that?" Jack asked.

"No. Estonia," she answered in all seriousness, which left Jack wondering whether he had heard her properly.

"Where?"

"Estonia."

"Estonia?"

"Yeah, you know, that place next to India," she said, still appearing to be totally serious, which gave Jack something to think about until he eventually realised.

"You mean that place next to Russia?"

"It's Russia, is it? Ah well, same difference," began Mandy. "I got it thrown in for free with that van load of jeans that I had delivered last week."

"Ah, so that's why it doesn't work. It's on a different electrical current. Just thank our lucky stars that the place hasn't gone up in flames. So, there's not much chance of a warranty or even a receipt of some sort then?" asked Jack.

"Bit of a silly question isn't, Jack?" she said. "Yes, I suppose it was really," Jack said, sighing heavily, still in disappointment.

"Jack?"

"Yes."

"I'm in trouble again," she said, full of sorrow, but which Jack didn't really pick up upon; he just remained interested in his newspaper and was happy just to make light of what he had just heard.

"You been trying to pick a fight with that copper who lives on the ground floor again? I've warned you; you'll go too far one day, and he'll nick you."

"It's not that, Jack. Anyway, he's up at Casualty being seen to," she said, quite casually.

"Casualty?" a shocked Jack said, hearing what he said jokingly now becoming a reality.

"Yeah, well that's what I heard. But he started it, Jack, honestly, he did, I promise you. But let's forget about him for now, okay. I'm in serious trouble, Jack, really don't know what I'm going to do," she said, as one or two genuine tears begin to emerge.

"At least three years by the sound of it," he was quick to respond with.

"Oh, Jack, please, forget about him, okay.

There were no witnesses, I saw to that," she told him. "Well, that's something I suppose. You may just get away with an insanity plea then." Jack again was very quick to respond with, but Mandy still saw nothing funny in what he was saying.

"Please, Jack, don't, I really am being deadly serious this time."

Jack, immediately put down his newspaper, because if the sad tone of her voice wasn't enough to convince him that there was something truly troubling her, but the very moment he finally turned around to see how deeply sad she looked, he instantly believed that she was in deep trouble and, quite simply, he couldn't bear to see her this upset.

"Hey, hey, come on you, it's not like you to get this upset over anything... Right, into the kitchen, now, cup of teatime, no arguing," he said with an authority that Mandy had no energy to argue with, and led her straight into the kitchen, sits her down at the table.

In what appeared to be no time at all, there was a hot, fresh, steaming cup of tea placed directly in front of her. And not forgetting the small plate of Jaffa Cakes, as he knew that she couldn't resist them, as he sat next her with a sympathetic ear, ready to listen.

"So, what's going on then?"

"Promise you won't laugh or tell me that I've been stupid or anything like that, Jack?" she said tearfully, before a much-needed sip of her tea, and being unable, no matter how she tried initially, to resist a Jaffa Cake, while her words left Jack feeling more than a touch offended.

"Hey, what sort of question is that then, huh? How long have we known each now? Well, come on, how long?"

"Since school."

"Exactly, since school, and that's got to be twenty years at least now. Maybe even more. And you should know by now that you can tell me absolutely anything without me judging you in any way at all. I'll always be here to help you if I can, you know that. So, let's try this again, shall we?

"What's going on, Mandy?"

"I'm sorry, Jack, didn't mean to doubt or offend you, honest I didn't… You've always been a good friend to me, I know that, but this is different, I don't really know where to start," she said, as Jack was quick to respond in a very forgiving tone.

PART TWO

The Boss

"Just try from the beginning, it's always been the best place to start, hasn't it?" he said to her. And he was right. Mandy knew that he was. So, after another sip of tea, and helping herself to another Jaffa Cake, she composed herself.

"Right, suppose there's no other way to say this. I've been having a secret affair with the boss. Must be for about six months now. Maybe a little longer."

Even though part of her was relieved that she had finally told someone, there was still a small part of her that felt ashamed about what she was doing, which was why she momentarily turned away from her friend and failed to spot Jack's eyebrows raised fully as he instantly began to look distinctly uncomfortable.

"Oh Jack, I feel not just stupid, but also downright foolish. Not just because he's married and all that, but I've also found out today from that Deirdre who runs the staff canteen that he's also been seeing Angie, Debbie, Sandra, and Alice as well."

"Oh," was all Jack could say to that.

"Oh Jack, I've been a right idiot. He promised me the world, he did. Said that he'd leave his wife for me and that we could and go and live anywhere that I wanted, and I'd never have to work again.

"But when I found out about the others, well, it hurt, I mean it really hurt, honestly felt like I was having my head kicked-in outside the pub on a Saturday night.

God, I feel so stupid because this isn't like me, not one little bit, 'cause normally, I'd spot his type a mile off and tell them to sling their hook before they get a slap.

"Oh Jack, I've really been such a fool."

"Oh," he replied.

"Wish that you'd stop just saying 'Oh'. Haven't you got anything else more constructive to say?" she asked, looking now straight at Jack, who seemed to be struggling to think of anything, constructive or otherwise, else to say as it just slipped out again'

"Oh."

"For Christ's sake, Jack! Oh, oh, oh, is that really all you've got to say? I mean, seriously, that's it? I've completely opened up to you, not only because you're without doubt my oldest friend, but I honestly believed that you'd be the best person to help me out with some advice or with anything practical that I could do next. "But all you can say is 'Oh'. Should have known better than to ask advice from a man, no matter how long I've known him. You're all bloody useless," she said, not just with a feeling of anger towards him, but more like let down by Jack, and she quickly woofed down another Jaffa Cake as Jack knew that he had to come up with something quick to help his friend out.

He suddenly said, "You need cheering up."

"No, I don't!" she immediately snapped in response.

"Yes, you do, you'll like this one," he confidently said to her.

"No, I won't" she had already decided.

"Listen, there were these three men in a pub one night…"

"I told you, no jokes, Jack! And I especially don`t want to hear any that involve men, okay, you got that?" There was no denying that Mandy had meant what she had just said.

"Okay, okay." Jack began to get the message loud and clear. "No jokes. But there is something that I need to ask you now."

"What!"

"Look, can you please clarify now that this boss you're talking about is in fact the same one that we both work for?"

"Yes."

"And this is the one that you've been having a secret affair with?" Jack asked, as Mandy soon felt no longer upset but was becoming more enraged by the second.

"Yes, Jack! I just said so, didn't I?"

"Right, and he's been seeing Angie, Debbie, Sandra, and Alice as well?" he asked in a calm and soothing tone, in the hope that it might just rub off on her. Not much chance of that happening just yet.

"Yes, he has. I should go around to his house right now with a carving knife and chop his bits off, as no court in the land would convict me after what he's done!" she said, looking like she just might carry out this threat at any second.

"Erm, think they just might," Jack began. "Probably with something like GBH or Assault with a Deadly Weapon maybe. So, please, think very carefully about doing anything like that, okay?" he said again, hoping his calming voice would have the correct effect on her, but yet again, his words weren't enough to bring her simmering temper down.

But another Jaffa Cake did help a little as she mercilessly devoured another one. Jack's recent questions were in fact leading to something and now, even though he knew that she still wasn't in best of moods, he had to tell her something. Regardless of any possible consequences.

"Right, well, seeing how this seems to the night for dishing out secrets, think I'd better reveal one that I've been keeping for a little while."

"What? You have a secret? Well, that's a novelty. Your life is usually an open book," a surprised Mandy then asked.

"Well, you'd better brace yourself for this then," he said.

"Brace myself? Well, now I'm intrigued, do tell," said Mandy, who is now all ears, taking another large drink from her tea.

"Well," Jack began nervously, "apart from Angie, Debbie, Sandra and Alice, the boss has been seeing someone else as well." He fully expected Mandy to be upset and angry on hearing this. And she didn't disappoint.

"WHAT? Another one? What the bloody hell is he doing? Having Viagra with his tea three times a day or something? Well, who is it, do you know? Oh, hang on, bet I know. It's that new cleaner, that slapper, Carol, you know the one, because I've often heard her mouthing off about her fantasies she has about her and the boss. And what she'd like to do with him."

"No, it's not her," Jack said, shaking his head, which now has Mandy racking her brains.

But after a minute or two, "Oh, I know. I bet it's that old dog, Karen, who works in the office, not long been there, you know the one. Tree-Trunk Legs, handkerchief for skirts, flat-chested and face like a bulldog chewing a wasp. Because more than once I've seen her making eyes and lusting after the boss."

"No, sorry, it's not her either," Jack said, which left Mandy utterly bewildered and not knowing who it could possibly be.

"Can't honestly think of anyone else," she said.

"Well, trust me, there is one other," Jack told her.

Consumed by curiosity, Mandy just had to ask, "Who is it?" as she is now sat on the very edge of her seat, in eager anticipation.

Jack took a long, slow, deep breath as he needed to compose himself, having no idea how Mandy was going to react to what he was about to tell her, but he knew that there was only one way to find out.

"Well, it's me."

PART THREE

The Jeans

Not a word was spoken between them for the next silent, and potentially very awkward, few minutes, as it could have taken a fork-lift truck to pick up Mandy`s jaw, which was now virtually touching the floor in shock of what she had just heard.

Jack remained exactly where he was, nervously awaiting her thoughts regarding his confession of not just who he was also having a secret affair, but about his sexuality, but probably the most important thing to him now was her acceptance. However, that would have to wait for a while as Mandy`s mobile began to ring, to which she answered.

"Hello, yeah, this is Mandy, who's this?"

"Oh, hello Les, didn't recognise your voice there. What can I do for you?" "You what?"

You got a three-door Corsa? Yeah, six months tax, insurance, three months and four previous owners and in decent nick?"

"Alright, how much?"

"Two grand, eh? Hmm. Tell you what I'll do for you, Les, I've got a van load of top quality jeans from Estonia that you'd probably make a few quid on if you fancy doing a straight swap?"

"You know, Estonia, that place next to Canada." "Same difference."

"I'll tell you what, Les, bring the car around tomorrow and I'll have a look at it and see if we can do a deal or something."

"Okay mate, see you tomorrow, bye."

Mandy then hung up and left her mobile on the table at the very moment that her jaw returned to virtually touching the floor and not being able to take her eyes off Jack as she eventually said, "I had absolutely no idea. Not a single bloody clue."

"About what?" Jack asked.

"About what? What do you mean about what? You know very well what I'm talking about. About you being gay," she said, as Jack acted all shy and coy before he finally answered.

"That was the general idea."

"What, that I shouldn't know?" she asked, feeling more than a touch offended by what he just said.

"That anyone shouldn't know. Well, not for now anyway," he said, as Mandy doesn't feel so offended for now.

However, she still had to ask, "Why not, Jack?"
"Because... Well, because and to be perfectly honest with you, until me and the boss got together, I still wasn't entirely convinced of it myself."

Mandy was still clearly struggling to come to terms to deal with what Jack had just told her, which would explain what she said next.

"Whoa, hang on a second here, so, he turned you gay? Or, oh, hang on again, did I turn him gay?" After a moment processing what she had just said, "Whoa, hang on a bloody second here, what am I saying? There's no way that I turned him gay. Not with the tricks that I know. Still confused though."

"Well, no… Not really. I think… Look, all I know is that I've had these feelings deep inside of me for a few years now. I've just never acted on them before," he explains to her, which did make things somewhat clearer for her.

"Until now that is," Mandy said.

"Well, yes," he said, as Mandy started to gently shake her head in disbelief.

"Still can't believe what I'm hearing," she began. "I'm gobsmacked and it's not very often that I get like this, but today, I have. Just can't believe it. After all the years that I've known you, I would never have guessed. I mean, if it is true, then you must admit that you are, without question, the straightest gay man that I've come across.

"You go rugby twice a week, and that's always followed by a night out with the lads, and look at all those girls that you've dated down the years.

"Let's think, oh yeah, there was that Cindy who works at the Corner Shop and that was less than a month ago. Then it was that Samantha before her, only a couple of weeks before her if my memory serves me right, and how about that Kathy then? Yeah, you know the one that I'm talking about, the one that you slept with just after New Year, and don't try and deny it because you both told me that it happened. And not forgetting all the others as well. You've even got a Page 3 Girl calendar on your bedroom wall, which I`ve seen you ogling at more than once."

"Okay, I know, I know all that, and I totally get that this is difficult for you to understand. Trust me, there's still plenty of times where I'm still struggling to understand it all myself. But I just had to find out who I really was. I just had to know.

"Now, don't get me wrong, `cause I never led any of these girls on. I always told them right from the start that I wasn't looking for any sort of commitment or even steady relationship so as no one got hurt. But as for Kathy, well, we'd both had a few drinks and been having such a great night, but it was like I said, I had to be sure. "I just had to know for certain whether I could or even wanted a physical relationship, not just with her but with any girl, and as it turned out, the answer is no. So, I had a good talk to her just as soon as I could and explained that I wasn't ready for a full-blown relationship, which she understood, and admitted that the wine just might have done a lot of our talking that night, so we parted on good terms. I think deep down that she appreciated me being honest with her rather than lead her a right merry old dance…"

"Does she know about, well, you know, about you being…"

"No, I never told her, didn't seem much point at the time, especially if I wasn't one hundred per cent certain of it myself. And I'd rather that she still didn't know for now, so if you do see her around, I'd be grateful if you didn't say anything just yet," he said, as Mandy continued to shake her head.

"Of course, I won't say anything, but I still can't believe it, after all this time," she said.

"I know, good actor, aren't I?" Jack somewhat proudly said.

"Good? That's an understatement if ever I've heard one. You should become a proper actor after that performance as you'd be winning Oscars left, right and centre in no time. But Jack, you still could have told me, you know that don't you?" she said.

"Yes, yes, Mandy, I do know that if I ever needed to, that I can confide in and trust you with anything that I may want to be kept secret, so please don't get annoyed with me or anything, but it was like I just said, I didn't want to say anything until I had no doubts about it myself. And now I don't. I know exactly who I am. But I'd still rather it remained between us, just for now anyway."

"Of course, I won't say nothing, Jack," she said reassuringly to him.

"Thanks for that."

"That's alright," Mandy began. "Anyway, forgive me for being a right old nosey cow, but I've got to ask, how exactly did you two get together in the first place? And when did it all start?" she asked, and Jack had no problems with telling her everything.

"Yeah okay, I'll tell you what happened... I was down the pub one night, must have been, what, not much more than two months ago now. The Royal Oak to be exact. It was the day after I'd found out that I got turned down for that Supervisor's job, remember? I was still feeling down about that because I really thought that I should have been given it and I just wanted to be by myself and have a good old sulk, just so I could get it out of my system. Then lo and behold, the boss walks in.

"I wasn't impressed at all when I set eyes on him, especially as he was all laughing and joking and buying all those stood by the bar drinks, whether he knew them or not.

"Found out later that he'd just secured that big hotel order that we're working on now, so he was more than flush. Yet again.

"After he'd paid for the latest round of drinks, it was then that he spotted me sat in the corner all alone, which like I said, was where I wanted to be. But he obviously decided that I needed some company, so totally uninvited, he literally bounced his way over and said hello. I said hello back, just to be polite, but I told him straight after that I was in no mood for company. But he wasn't taking a blind bit of notice of that, so he took it upon himself to buy me a pint, which he puts on the table right in front of me, before sitting down right next to me. Well, I then thought to myself, I suppose if he insists, one pint with him won't hurt, especially seeing how he bought it.

"Before I knew what was really happening, we were sat there chatting away like we were old mates or something, but I did have to mention to him how disappointed I was that I didn't get that Supervisor's job, which he understood that I would be, as he then began reassuring me by saying things like, 'Don't be too downhearted' and 'Your time will come', and do you know something, Mandy? Strangely, I truly began to believe him."

"It was the weirdest thing, that the more we chatted, and obviously had a few more drinks, which he was still more than happy to pay for, the more that some sort of chemistry was really brewing between us, and before I think that either of us knew what was really happening, well…"

"One thing led to another I take it" Mandy deduced.

"Well, yeah," said Jack.

"Oh," said Mandy, as neither one had anything else to say for now.

PART FOUR

The Sheep

The kitchen fell silent while they both pondered very seriously about the accidental predicament that they had found themselves in.

It was Jack who eventually broke the ice with, "He was crap, wasn't he?"

Mandy just raises an eyebrow as she knows exactly to what he is referring to.

"You think so?" she asked.

"Well, I know that it was my first time a man and all that, but he still didn't do a lot for me," said Jack.

"Well, being totally honest and frank about it myself, I have had better myself," Mandy then said. "I dare say that you have," Jack was quick to point out.

And what exactly do you mean by that?" Mandy asked.

"Now, hang on now you," Jack said, knowing only too well that he had to choose his next few words very carefully. "I don't mean to say that you've been putting yourself about a lot or anything like that, I'd never say anything like that about you, it's just that I've heard, on more than one occasion, even from you after a couple of tequilas, that you're, let's say, pretty broad-minded when it comes to the bedroom department."

Mandy couldn't help but agree.

"It's like I've always said, that if it pretty much stays in the bedroom, and both are willing to it, then I don't see why anyone should be shy, and I do actively encourage, most of the time, just about any form of experimentation," she said.

Jack answered, "Suppose that's fair enough."

"Glad you said that," Mandy said, "because there`s something that I'd like to ask you." "Okay, fire away."

"Right then. When you and the boss were, you know, together like…"

"Yes."

"Did you ever get the bondage gear out?"

Jack was slightly taken aback by this question, as Mandy sat there, keen to know.

"No. Why, did you?" asked Jack, and as he did so, Mandy`s eyes immediately lit up.

"Oh God, yes. Yes, we did. I mean, I had to help him to begin with as he was new to all of it and the gear, but once it was on, ooooo, the feel of all that leather clutching tightly against my skin, particularly between my thighs that makes me go all…"

"Yes, I think we get the general idea of how it makes you go thank you very much," Jack suddenly said as Mandy then came back into the room.

"Whoops, sorry, always get a bit carried away when I start to think of things like that," she said with a cheeky smile.

"That's alright," Jack began. "Can I ask you something now?"

"Yeah, of course you can."

"Alright then, so when you and the boss were together, apart from the bondage sessions obviously, err, did you ever get the sheep impressions?"

Even regardless of her broad-minded attitude and willingness to openly experiment, this was something that Mandy had never heard of before.

"What!" she exclaims.

Jack said again, quite calmly, "Sheep impressions."

"Hang on a second here, sheep impressions, seriously? How the hell did that all come about then?"

Mandy asked, dying to know.

"Well, to be absolutely truthful, I'm not exactly sure myself," Jack began. "There we were in bed one night with me on top doing my best, 'cause as I said before, this was my first time with any man, and totally out of the blue, and for no reason at all, well, none that I can still not think off, he just started going, 'Baa, Baa', which I will happily admit right here and now, did puzzle me at first."

"Yes, I can see how it would. Would have really puzzled me as well, as it's the first time that I've heard of anything like that," Mandy said.

"I'm telling you, it did puzzle me, almost threw me off my game as well because I distinctly remember at the time whether I'd might have pulled Shaun the Sheep. Which led me to another dilemma," he said.

"Which was?" Mandy asked utterly intrigued by this. "Well, do I threaten him with mint sauce in order to try and shut him up, or do I give a chorus of Old Macdonald in order to try and, you know, give him that bit of extra sensual pleasure," he told her.

Mandy just couldn't help but start to giggle before asking, "So, what did you do then?"

"As it turned out, nothing, because totally unexpectedly, we both heard the front door open as his wife came home a lot earlier that we both thought she would."

"So, I had to quickly and quietly get dressed, then it was out of the window and down the drainpipe and leg it out of there as fast as I possibly could," Jack told her. The last part especially, Mandy found highly amusing. "Aww, she would spoil it by coming home early, and just when it was getting really interesting as well," she said through her laughter, as Jack looked at her quite sternly.

"It's not that funny," he said.

"I'm sorry, I know that I shouldn't be laughing really, but you've got to be honest, Jack, it is comical. It's like something out of those old British, saucy, comedy films, you know the ones I mean.

"Where the young man gets seduced by a lonely older woman type who just wants some fun while the husband is away, and then halfway through, comes home earlier than expected and the boy has to try and not get caught," she said, still through the laughter, as Jack remained completely stone-faced about it all.

Mandy was beginning to calm down a lot now. In fact, she began to feel so calm, it was if someone had flipped a switch to turn her laughter off and become almost as stone-faced as Jack now was.

"In fact, you're absolutely right, Jack, I shouldn`t be laughing about any of this at all," she then said in a most serious tone of voice.

"Yeah, you're right, Mandy, we shouldn't be laughing really," he said, starting to see the funny side but not at all sensing Mandy's more serious tone for now. But he was soon about to.

"No Jack, I'm serious, we really shouldn't be laughing about any of this."

"What's wrong? You were all but in fits of laughter only a minute or so ago, so what's up with you now?" a very confused Jack asked.

"Well," said Mandy, taking a deep breath to compose herself and then slowly breath out. "Well, seeing how this seems to be a night of revealing secrets, I've got one more for you."

"What's that then?" he asked.

"Ah well, just better off coming out and saying it I suppose. Jack, I'm pregnant."

"You're what?" Jack screams, as he literally jumps out of his chair in amazement, scarcely believing what he had just heard. "Really?" he then asked.

"Yes, really."

"What, are you okay? How far gone are you? Do you want a drink or something? Or how about a nice lay down? Get some sleep, surely that'll do you good," he said, acting like a Mother Hen, but which Mandy found very endearing.

"Oh Jack, stop fussing, will you? Honestly, you're like an old woman at times, you really are… And I'm just over ten weeks gone now," she told him, smiling sweetly at her oldest and dearest friend, which had the desired effect (if that was her intention) of calming him down as he then took a deep breath.

"The boss, I mean, I take it that he is…"

"The father, is that what you were about to say? Then yes, yes, he is," she told him as they both go quiet, not exactly sure what to say next.

Jack finally asked, "So, what are you going to do?" Mandy remains momentarily quiet while considering her answer.

"Really not sure yet, Jack" she answered truthfully.

"Well, you know that if you ever need anything, anything at all, then you only have to ask, okay?" Jack genuinely asked as Mandy endears to him even more.

"Yes, I know, thanks Jack."

"Hey, what are friends for… There's no doubt?" he asked.

"No, no doubts. Doctor confirmed it this morning," she said.

"Bloody hell, Mandy. What's going to happen next?"

"I don't know, Jack… I just don't know," she said, as they both remained at the table, thinking hard about what maybe Mandy should do next, but after a minute or two, Jack thought it might be a good idea to change the subject for now.

"Look, I hope that you don`t mind me asking…"
"Asking what?"

"Well, seeing how I've told how me and the boss first got together. I was…"

"Wondering what happened with me?"

"Well, yes," he said, as Mandy clearly had no objection telling him.

"Yeah, okay then. To be honest though, not much to tell. Suppose you could say it's the same old story of poor and stupid girl being swept off her feet by a right old charmer.

"It all started soon after me and Freddie had finished. Or should I say when he ended things. Still find it hard to believe that he done that, as I really thought that we could have made a good go of things, and possibly could have had a good future together. Certainly, got that wrong, didn't I?"

"Anyhow, there I was at work one day, outside in the smoking shelter, and must have looked a right sad, old cow, feeling all sorry for myself, when suddenly, the boss appeared and noticed me straight away.

"He didn't mess about. He came straight over, lit up a cigar and began asking me what was wrong. 'And don't try and pretend that there's nothing wrong 'cause I can quite clearly see that there is,' he'd said.

"There was no fooling him, so I told him what had happened between me and Freddie and instantly, he began to say how sorry he was to hear it and he offered to help if he could in anyway, which I suppose was nice of him. We just started talking about this and that until, and completely out of the blue, he started paying me compliments and saying things like how any bloke would be lucky to have a girl like me and how he'd always thought I was a very pretty girl.

"And I cannot tell a lie, I was flattered, very flattered in fact, couldn't help it, because let's face facts, with his good looks and seeing how successful he is, there's no doubting that he's had more than his fair share of women over the years.

"What came as even more of a shock to me, apart from all the compliments that he was still paying me, was when he suddenly asked me out. Just as friends to begin with, he insisted, but at the time, I didn't care if it was just as friends or if he wanted more."

"It just felt so nice to feel wanted, or even desired if you want, because that's how he was making me feel right there and then. Obviously, I said yes, and that's about it. We saw each other every Wednesday after that." "Really? I was every Tuesday," said Jack, as Mandy appeared to drift off into her own little dreamworld as fond memories came flooding back to her.

"It was flowers and champagne on a regular basis, and no expense was ever spared."

"Oh right, he once bought me a pint and a packet of crisps," said Jack.

"He often took me to the theatre, and he took me to all the best shows. Even on occasion up to London's West End."

"Really? Well, that's nice. We once rented a DVD from Blockbusters, which I had to pay for," was Jack's next remark, looking more than a touch disgruntled by what Mandy was telling him.

She then went on to say, "And I lost count of how many times when all I had to do was send him a text or even give him a quick ring, and he would have his chauffeur drive me around in his Rolls Royce. Even if it was just to pick me up from Asda with the weekly shop." "By the way, I borrowed your Rollerblades," Jack then told her as they both, seemingly right on cue, sighed heavily.

Mandy said, "Yup, he really swept me off my feet."

"Same old story then," Jack said.

"Yeah, I suppose it is. He even said that he'd take me abroad once," said Mandy, much to Jack's surprise.

"Did he?" he asked

"Oh yeah. To the Algarve, said we could go just after Christmas Day, get a spot or two of winter sun to get the tan started."

"Bloody hell. The Algarve, eh, very nice I must say, especially as I couldn't get a weekend at Butlins out of him. But I take it he didn't," he said, which brought some deep-rooted anger out of Mandy to the surface.

"No, he bloody didn't. Every time I asked him about it, it was always how it was never the right time to leave the factory or some other excuse that he could think of."

"Oh, so that's why you were in such a bad mood when we were watching *Elf* last Christmas. Thought it was a bit weird at the time, 'cause you usually love watching that film," said Jack.

Mandy then storms, "He took advantage of me!"

"And me," Jack quickly adds.

Mandy continues, "When I was at my lowest and most vulnerable."

"Same here," said Jack, as Mandy began to realise. "Yes, that's right, he did, didn't he? So, it's fair to say that he's done the dirty on both of us," she said, to which Jack couldn't help but agree.

"Yes, yes, you could say that, couldn't you? Anyway, there were these three men in a pub one night…"

PART FIVE

The Row

Just like she had already told him, and not that long ago, the last thing that Mandy wanted to hear right now was any of Jack's jokes, especially if they involved men in any shape or form, which was clear by the expression on her face the very second that Jack began attempting to tell this one again.

It was with a sense of relief that her mobile then rang again, as she didn't hesitate in answering it.

"Hello, yes."

"Oh, hello Dave, how's things? Been a while since I heard from you.

What's up mate?"

"You've got a complete set of patio furniture, excellent condition, along with a brand-new gas barbecue that is also in excellent condition, and that you're willing to let me have at half its recommended price?"

"Oh really?"

"What's the catch, Dave? If it's in that good condition, you should flog it for what it's really worth." "Oh, she doesn`t like it and you want a quick sale to free up space in the garden for something else? Alright Dave, I believe you, thousands probably wouldn't, but let me ask you something, mate."

"Now, in case you've forgotten, which it looks like you have, I live on the top floor of a small block of flats, which has no communal garden, so why would I want anything like that?"

"You what? Oh, I'm sorry, Dave, mate, didn't hear you properly. Got other things on my mind right now. Do I know of anyone who would be interested?

Well, no one springs to mind just now…"

"Oh yeah, of course I'll let you know if I do hear of someone, but I'm glad you phoned, Dave, 'cause I've heard that you're setting up a market stall, is that right?"

"Oh really? That's even better then because I might just have something That'll suit you down to the ground."

"A van load of top-quality jeans from Estonia. Dave, wouldn't lie to you, these are of such quality; you'd think they were made by Wrangler and you could easily make a good profit on them."

"You know Estonia."

"Go across the English Channel, carry on straight through France, then turn right at the Spanish border." "You what… Same difference. Anyway, you interested?"

"Alright mate, you have a think about it but don't take too long 'cause I'm telling you someone is going to make a nice little profit of these and seeing how you're an old mate, I'd like it to be you. Okay, Dave? Pardon? What's that?"

"You were wondering about what exactly?"

"Oh, do I know, Dave?"

"Ah, you want some more DVDs, do you?" "Yes, I know the ones that you mean."

"The ones solely intended for private viewing. Yours, to be exact."

"Yes Dave, it'll stay our little secret, alright. I`ll see what I can get hold of and it'll be the usual price, okay."

"That's alright, cheers Dave, bye."

After hanging up, she put her mobile back down on the kitchen table with a surprising amount of force, which Jack thought was a tad unnecessary, and suddenly, and what seemed to be for some unknown reason, she was clearly looking rather more upset than she was earlier when he found out about her affair with the boss.

Now, he thought that it was to assume that this was nothing really to do with the fact that she still couldn't yet get rid of this van load of Estonian jeans, as not being able to pull off a deal has, in the past, caused her to become somewhat agitated.

So, and without trying to tell any of his jokes, he thought he would try and cheer her up.

"Hey, come on, don't worry about it, for now. I'm sure that you`ll find a mug… sorry, I mean a buyer for those jeans soon enough, come on, chin up," he told her in all seriousness, while Mandy just looked straight back at him with not one flicker of emotion.

"You know something, Jack," she began, "right now, I really couldn't care less about those jeans, and do you know why that is? It's because I've been sat here thinking that how dare he cheat on me. I mean, it was bad enough it was with all those other girls, but with you as well!

He really must have been scraping the bottom of the barrel then, "she said, hissing her contempt for Jack who was understandably taken slightly aback, but thought it best to remain calm for now. "Right, I'm going to put that down to not only of the shock of what we've both found out tonight, but also, in your condition right now, your hormones could very well be all over the place, and I get that totally," he told her, doing his absolute utmost not to appear patronising in anyway.

"You can put it any way that you want, okay, you still make me sick," she said, still hissing at him with utter contempt.

"Oi you," he said, not liking what he had heard for the second time within only a matter of seconds.

"Oi you? Oi you? What do you mean, oi you? Just who the hell do you think you are with the oi you, huh?"

"Think that you can talk to me like I'm some sort of skivvy, well? Think that you're better than me yet again? Like you always did!"

"No, I didn't" Jack said, still not understanding what on earth had prompted this attack on him. An attack that for now seemed relentless.

"Yes, you did! Oh, yes, you did! Even when we were at school, you just loved to lord it over me, like the fact you were always top of the class while I struggled near the bottom, while you were never in trouble and I lost count of the times that I was in detention, always thinking that you were something special. And as for your mum!"

She yelled at him, and if he wasn't miffed before about this attack, her last comment regarding his mum had him totally scratching his head.

"What the hell has my mum got to do with all of this?" he asked.

"Oh, come off it, Jack," she began, "it was always `my precious Jack this, my precious Jack that. Oh, look everyone, my Jack has topped the class yet again. Which is no big surprise really, is it? He'll go far when he leaves school, no doubt about that. Also, seeing what a handsome-looking boy he is, he shouldn't have any problems finding a girl.

But whether he can find a girl that's good enough for him, well, that's a different matter entirely.' Really used to turn my stomach every time I heard it. But look at you now, hardly a captain of industry are you?"

"No, just a lowly and common factory worker. And I wonder if mummy would be proud of her special little boy if she found out that his only love life is a dirty and sordid affair with the boss?"

It didn't matter how much Jack cared and loved Mandy, because he truly did, and nothing, for him, would ever change that fact, but that still didn't mean that he had to sit there and take any of this from her. He had no intention of doing that, so, he began fighting back with a sarcastic comment.

"Oh, you bitch," which he knew deep down would more than likely rile her. And he was right.

"Bitch? Oh, bitch, am I?" she shouted at him. Jack calmly answered, "Amongst other things."

"Oh, really? Like what then? Come on, like what? Let's hear it then, Jack. That's if you've got the guts to say it?" she demanded to know, and Jack wasn't going to be intimidated by her anytime soon.

"Okay then, how about scrounger and a tart?"

Mandy couldn't believe her ears and suddenly felt a rage inside her that she had rarely felt before.

"What did you just call me?"

"What, are you deaf? You heard. Scrounger. Because let's face facts, it's only my name on the tenancy, so this is my flat that you're living in, and at a reduced rent, I might add, and why is it?

"Oh yeah, to help you recover your losses from that stupid batch of Chinese perfume that you bought, remember? What is it you said? A mystical and exotic scent of the Orient, and what was it called again? Oh yeah, Long Poo. Rather apt name, wasn`t it? Considering that's what it smelt like. A real seller that turned out to be, eh? Not!

"And now look what you've got yourself stuck with. Jeans from Estonia. Seriously. Estonia! Have they suddenly become the world`s leading manufacturer of denim, huh? Are the owners of Levi's suddenly quaking in their boots as we speak, scared of the threat that Estonia poses to them and their trade, well? And as for tart, well, that pretty much goes without saying, because if you looked up the word promiscuous in the dictionary, it would say 'See Mandy Cartwright', wouldn't it? Now with your cheap and tacky affair with the boss, you can add that to your little black book, or in your case, should I say telephone directory?"

"I should have known really. Should have guessed that something was up. I mean you, going to a Quiz Night every Wednesday at The Fox and Hound? You? Doing a Pub Quiz? I still haven't forgotten when we were watching Chris Tarrant on the telly a few weeks ago and he asked that bloke to name The Three Musketeers, and you shouted out Larry, Curly, and Mo, didn`t you? Bet if it was a question regarding the world's oldest profession, you would have got it right without even thinking about it, wouldn't you, eh?"

By now though, Mandy had heard more than enough, and she began her fight back with, "You can talk, eh, every Tuesday, 'Oh, I'll be late home after rugby training, going out for a few beers with the lads.' Really? At least now I know what sort of scrum down you were working on, eh? You make me sick!"

To which Jack instantly retaliated with, "And as for all these stupid, dodgy deals that you keep coming up with, just who do you think you are, some sort of Del Boy?"

To which Mandy calmly, and with quite a degree of smugness, answered, "Well, rather this flat be known for having a Del Boy than a Gay Boy."

"You What?!" a now outraged Jack screamed, as then, completely unexpectedly, they were saved by the bell. The doorbell to be exact.

The doorbell had a clear impatient tone to it as it rang for the second time, and soon after, the third, but neither Jack nor Mandy were taking any notice of it for now, as they stood at opposites ends of the kitchen table, glaring and snarling at each other like two bare-knuckle fighters just waiting for the opening bell so that they can start tearing each other to pieces.

"That'll be for you," Jack snarled.

"Oh yeah, how do you know that?" Mandy asked through gritted teeth.

"Let's just say that I'm a little psychic," Jack said, still snarling away, as he now had his fists clenched tightly as he possibly could.

Mandy once again came over all smug, as she had now turned into 'Little Miss Attitude'.

"What, as well as being a faggot?"

"You What?! Dare you to say that again, go on, I dare you!" he shouts at her, showing one of his clenched fists, but if he thought that doing this would in some way intimidate or even scare her, he couldn't be more wrong.

The doorbell rang again and Mandy, still very much 'Little Miss Attitude' and looking back over her shoulder as she began making her way out of the kitchen, happily said, "Well, alright then, faggot."

PART SIX

The Police

She continued through the living room and towards the front door, and no sooner than she opened it, there was quite a surprise, as two very smartly dressed men were standing there with more than an air of authority about them.

"Excuse me, miss, so sorry to disturb you, but I'm Detective Sergeant Connor and this is my colleague, D.C. Rea. We're looking for a Miss Mandy Cartwright," said D.S. Connor.

"Excuse me, sorry, but what did you say your names were again?" asked Mandy, just wanting to make sure that she heard correctly the first time.

"I'm Detective Sergeant Connor and this is my colleague, Detective Constable Rea," D.S. Connor happily told her again, and no sooner had he done so, but the cogs of Mandy's mischievous mind started to turn as she felt sure that she could come up with some sort of joke name for them as she began to start thinking aloud.

"Connor and Rea, Connor and Rea... Connorrea, Connorea," she repeats a few more times before declaring, "I've got it!"

"Got what, miss?" asked D.C. Rea.

"Gonorrhoea!" she happily declared. "Oh, I'm very sorry to hear that, miss," said D.C. Rea before turning to his superior. "First time that I've seen anyone happy about getting that, Sarge."

"No, not me, you two. When you put your names together, it sounds like gonorrhea. You got it now? Bet all the lads down at the station have a right laugh at you two from the very moment that you both walk in."

Both D.S. Connor and D.C. Rea first looked at each other before their heads slumped down towards their own chests and sighed, sounding deflated that someone else has figured out what happens when their names are put together, as they prepare themselves for even more ridicule to come their way.

Mandy's temper had by now somewhat magically disappeared and was replaced by her giggling like an adolescent, before she continues, "So, what branch are you two with then? The newly formed STD Squad, is it?"

"Yes, miss, very funny, but please don't bother trying to think up anymore because I can assure you that as far as our names are concerned, we've heard the lot, and a lot more besides as well," said D.S. Connor, which was a point that D.C. Rea was quick to add to.

"Yes, that's right, miss, heard the lot, even the ones that have nothing to do with our names, like, there were these three men in a pub one night…"

"Yeah, that's right, even that one, so, if you don't mind, we'd like to get on with what we came here to do," said D.S. Connor.

"Which is?" asked Mandy.

"Well, we've come here tonight looking for a Miss Mandy Cartwright. Does she live here?" D.S. Connor asked.

Mandy had absolutely no fear in telling him, "Why yes, she does, you're looking at her." Which pleased D.S. Connor the very moment he heard it.

"Oh great, well, if you do not mind then, Miss Cartwright, we'd like to ask you a few questions," he said.

"Really, like what exactly?" Mandy asked, as she rolled up the sleeves of her jumper to her elbows before folding her arms and looked steely-eyed. She was now ready for anything that they could possibly throw at her. "It's about two separate incidents actually," D.S. Connor said. "Firstly, regarding an alleged assault that took place earlier on today in this very building on a P.C. Brian Winters, and secondly, we are investigating a consignment of jeans that we believe have been smuggled in from Estonia."

Mandy didn't say anything for now. She stayed exactly where she was and decided to find out what sort of men she was up against, as she fixed her steely eyes right into the eyes of D.S. Connor, who had absolutely no intention of backing down as he stared right back at her with a now puffed-out chest and rolling his shoulders back, all set for action. Mandy then turned her attention to D.C. Rea, who, the moment his eyes met Mandy's, decided that he wanted no part of her, and, as discreetly as he possibly could, edged his way backwards about a foot or so, which she loved seeing him do.

He then asked, "Do you think that we'll need backup for this one, Sarge?"

D.S. Connor was not only taken aback by this question, but he was clearly quite insulted by it also. "Backup?" he said. "Backup? Are you seriously trying to tell me that two strong blokes like us couldn't manage a mere slip of a girl like Miss Cartwright, if it were at all required to do so?"

"Sorry Sarge. It's just that when I saw P.C. Winters down at Casualty, well, he wasn't exactly a pretty sight," said D.C. Rea very apologetically.

"Well let's be honest now, he never was to begin with, was he?" D.S. Connor said quite forcefully before continuing. "And he's a total wimp. How he ever got took on by the force in the first place is beyond me, it really is. Can't even protect himself, let alone any member of the public."

"Yes, I suppose you're right there, Sarge," said D.C. Rea, still very apologetically.

"Of course, I'm right! So, if you've quite finished asking me stupid questions regarding backup, can we continue?" D.S. Connor seriously wanted to know, as D.C. Rea just nodded and edged himself as little further back in the process.

His superior continued, saying, "So, Miss Cartwright, if you have no objections, would you mind answering some questions?"

"Got a warrant?" Mandy asked, being quite direct with him.

"Do I need one?" D.S. Connor asked in very much the same manner.

"Well, you do if you want anything out of me," Mandy fired back at him, to which D.S. Connor only had one answer.

"Or we could just arrest you now and take you down the station to answer our questions," he strongly hinted at, as well as seemingly very keen to do, but Mandy, showing no fear whatsoever, was happy to stand her ground.

"Arrest me, eh? Oh really? You and what army?" she said with a grin, as unbeknown to D.S. Connor, D.C. Rea had discreetly edged himself to being exactly behind his superior.

He now said, "Shall we call for backup now, Sarge?" Clearly now realising that he could not rely on his colleague and that there was no way that Mandy was going to back down, D.S. Connor knew that he had to call upon all his years of experience to try and calm the very rapidly escalating tension.

"Right, okay, I think that we should all just calm down, alright. All we want to do, Miss Cartwright, is to ask you a few questions, nothing more, nothing less, and we certainly didn't come here with the intention of arresting you or anyone else for that matter. Isn't that right, D.C. Rea?"

"Yes Sarge," he answered, but stayed directly behind his superior where he felt the safest.

Mandy deliberated what she was going to say next. "You just want to ask me a few questions without any trouble then, do you?" she began by saying. "Right, here's what I want to do. Do you see that man sat there?" she asked, pointing directly through the living room and at the kitchen table, where Jack was still sat as he gave them a friendly wave and D.S. Connor nodded back in acknowledgement.

"Right, now, he just happens to be not only my oldest but also my dearest friend in the entire world, ever, and right at the very moment that you disturbed us, we were in the middle of a very deep and very meaningful conversation that could quite possibly turn out to change both our entire lives at some point.

"So, the last thing that we need right now is a pair of clowns like you two coming around here, wanting to ask utterly pointless questions to things that I absolutely know nothing about! Is this what I pay my taxes for, I don't think so!

"Maybe if muppets like you two would concentrate on trying to catch real criminals rather than waste everyone's time on bothering decent people like me and my friend, then just maybe the crime rate would begin to come down and people around here will begin to feel a lot safer.

"Right, so, if you've got nothing else to say, I would very much like to re-join my friend and continue with our conversation without any more interruptions. So, both of you now, SOD OFF!! And don't even think of ringing this doorbell again. Got that? Good!"

Mandy was very clear about what she had just said before taking great pleasure in slamming the door.

Mandy's fingers moved just as fast as they possibly could to ensure that the chain was now securely on, and the very second that she had done this, Jack called out. "Do you feel better for that?"

She didn't answer him, not because she did indeed feel a lot better for having a rant at gonorrhea, but she was now suddenly consumed with guilt. Guilt of the way that she had treated Jack before they were interrupted.

She turned to look at Jack, who gave her a very approving thumbs-up for what she had just done, but that still didn't make her feel any better as she lowered her head and made her way slowly back to the kitchen, not being able to look at him as he just sat at the table, not saying a word.

PART SEVEN

The Jaffas

He watched her enter the kitchen and pick up the plate that she originally used and go to the cupboard and replenish the plate with what turns out to be the last of the Jaffa Cakes, and after making them both a hot fresh cup of tea, she ensured that he had the plate as she mumbled, "Peace offering?"

"Peace offering?" asked Jack.

"Yes, peace offering. Oh, come on, Jack, we both know why. You're not going to make me spell it out, are you?"

"Err, well, yes, I am actually," Jack said with a smug grin on his face as he took one Jaffa Cake, which he very much enjoyed, and then sat back in his chair waiting to hear what Mandy had to say next. And he hoped it would be good, as she certainly owed him a decent apology, which he knew only too well.

"Oh Jack, what can I say? Sorry doesn't seem to be enough as you really didn't deserve me going at you like that. But I am really truly sorry. Maybe you were right, maybe it was my hormones raging all over the place, but whatever it was, I still shouldn't have taken it out on you.

"I'm really sorry, Jack," she said, pouring out her heart to him and seeking his forgiveness, but Jack didn't say anything to begin with. He had no intention to. He just helped himself to another of her peace offering, which again he enjoyed.

"Well, aren't you going to say anything?" Mandy then asked. "I'm really sorry, Jack, honestly I am. Come on, say something," she said, with just a hint of desperation, looking for the forgiveness that she craved.

Not only did Jack want to keep her hanging on. He also wanted to hate her right now, truly wanted to hate her, as he knew only too well that he didn't deserve not just the attack from her but also, the `faggot' comment was uncalled for. But he just couldn't do that for too long, especially as he knew that she did regret what she did, truly regretted it.

"Look, maybe I shouldn't have said those things about you either, so let's forget about the whole thing, okay, and put it down to the shock of what we've both found out tonight that has made us say all these things... And if you need an alibi for earlier today, just ask, okay, I'll happily provide one for you," he offers, before pushing the plate of Jaffa Cakes towards her, but ensuring that he took another one for himself first. Obviously.

"Thanks Jack, I don't deserve you at times, I really don't," she said in all honestly.

"That's true."

"But don't worry about thinking about making up an alibi for me. It's great of you to offer but I won't be needing be one," she assures him.

This instantly sparked Jack's curiosity as he asked, "Oh yeah, how come?"

"Because if the worst does in fact come to the worst, I shall just have to have a discreet word with the Chief Constable and explain to him that I just happen to have in my possession certain pictures of him and a certain prostitute who's dressed up as Helga the German Barmaid. Complete with blonde wig and pigtails and frilly, low-cut dress, which shows an ample amount of cleavage, while he's dressed up as Franz, a local businessman, in the full lederhosen, including that silly, little hat that has a feather poking out of the side of it."

"Because I can guarantee you, Jack, he won't want any of those pictures seeing the light of day anytime soon," she told him with a grin, as Jack's eyes lit up.

"What pictures? Can I see them? Oh, go on, show me," he asked excitedly in hope.

"I'll show you some other time," she said, much to his disappointment.

"Oh, go on, Mandy, let's have a look. I could do with a good laugh," he said.

"No Jack, not just yet, but I promise that I'll show you soon, okay," she said, as Jack then suddenly realised something.

"Whoa, whoa, whoa, hang on a second here, where exactly did you get them from?"

"From Beth, you know, the redhead who lives just behind Asda," she explained.

"Oh, that Beth, yes, I know her. I'm with you now. Christ, haven't seen her around for months. I take it she's still working as a…"

"Oh God, yeah, of course she is. She won't be giving that up for a while yet. Still got a bit of life left in her yet. It's her in the pictures dressed as Helga," she went on to tell him.

"And she really won't mind you using them?" He asked.

"No, of course not. That's why she gave them to me, as a little, let's say, get out jail free card, just in case I ever needed them, as I helped her out with not only a new microwave but a few quid when she was short   a few months ago. Kept a few for herself obviously, just in case she needs them," Mandy said, which only whetted Jack's appetite for seeing them even more."

"Oh, go on, Mandy, let's see them, please? If you do, then I'll tell you the one about the three men in a pub one night," he said.

"Honestly, Jack, I promise, I'll show you another time, alright. Just not really in the mood   right now," she said, genuinely sounding like she would keep this promise, but Jack still couldn't help but be disappointed.

"Oh, okay then, spoilsport," he then said, as Mandy quickly changed the subject.

"And thanks again for offering to give me an alibi, you really didn't have to do that, especially after the way that I'd just treated you, for no good reason."

"Hey, don't worry about it 'cause it's just like I said earlier, what are friends for?" he said with a friendly smile.

"Let's be honest about this, Jack, you've always been much more than a friend to me. We both know that. Ever since all those years ago on that day after school when that gang of boys were going to beat me up because they thought I'd nicked all their bikes and chucked them in the river, then out of nowhere, you appeared, my very own knight in shining armour and stuck up for me," which was a tale that they were both happy to recall.

Jack then said modestly, "That wasn't a problem. I mean, five lads picking on one girl. Just about any lad would have done the same thing, and anyway, I know that you didn't do it because you told me that you didn't, isn't that right?" said Jack, as he couldn't help but notice how suspiciously guilty Mandy suddenly looked.

"Well…"

"Well, what?" asked Jack.

"I always meant to tell you."

"Tell me what, Mandy? Oh my God, you did chuck their bikes in the river, didn't you?" Jack suddenly realised, which Mandy couldn't deny anymore.

"Well, they did start it, Jack," she protested. "Oh really, how?"

"Because the day before, when I was walking home by myself, minding my own business, they thought that it would be funny to knock me down as they rode past me, then nick my schoolbag and throw it into a nearby skip."

Jack very much had his suspicions. "Really, Mandy?"

"Honestly, Jack, I promise that I'm telling the truth this time," Mandy said, pleading her innocence, which Jack gave some serious deliberation to.

"Okay, Mandy, I believe you, even though I think probably thousands wouldn't," he began by saying. "Because I know deep down that you don't go looking for that sort of trouble, but it does have a habit of finding you."

"Yeah, that's true," Mandy couldn't help but agree. "Still, when I think back to that day, I still find it hard to believe that they all ran away when I confronted them, as I would easily bet that any one of them could have easily beaten me up," he said.

"And do you know why they all ran off?" Mandy began. "Gutless, all of them. Only big and hard when it came to a girl who was by herself."

"Well, obviously, and also, thankfully for me, eh?"

"And ever since that day, I've always known that if anything got out of hand, and if I ever needed that special someone to help me out, then you'd always be there," she positively gushed.

"And do you know why that is?" he asked. "No."

"It's because yes, you can be tough, but you're nowhere near as tough or as clever as you like to think you are at times," he told her, which Mandy was somewhat dubious about.

"Aren't I, Jack?" she asked.

He then answered her point blankly, "No, Mandy, you're not," and there was no more argument about it.

PART EIGHT

The Baby

"You're right again, Jack, as usual. You had me sussed out from that very day, didn't you, eh?"

Jack couldn`t argue with that fact. "That's true," he said.

Mandy continued, "And again, I'm sorry for having a go at you, and I also didn't mean to have a go at your mum either. She's alright really."

"Yes, I suppose that she is. Apart from the fact that she can be the biggest pain in the neck going when she wants to be," he said, as Mandy remembered something else.

"And I've always said that she was dead right about what she used to say about us. Or indeed, she sometimes still does."

"Oh yeah, what's that then?" Jack asked.

"That even though she wasn't entirely impressed by me when we first started hanging out together – she'd always thought that I would lead you astray – but she did say something once that I'll never forget. That there was something very special between us."

Jack deliberately took a moment to think back to this time before he answered, "Yes, she did say that didn't she?"

"And she always used to like making a fuss over you, didn't she, eh?" Mandy said, remembering fondly. "Fuss? It was nothing less than embarrassing most of the time. Especially all those times outside the school gates. Having my clothes checked as well as having her seeing if I'd combed my hair properly and had a clean handkerchief in my pocket and doing all this in front of everybody. Suppose I should have been grateful that she didn't check that my underpants were clean there and then."

"Aww, she just wanted you to look your best, that's all. Deep down, she didn't mean any harm," Mandy said. "Yes, I suppose you're right about that," Jack reluctantly agreed, before continuing, "It's strange though, but when I was around there the other week, and as per usual, she was fussing around me, out of completely nowhere, and God knows why, she hands me this book about parenting and strongly suggests that I read it. `Isn't it about time that considered raising your own family? You're not getting any younger, are you?' Charming, I first thought, before thinking to myself that she's going to have a long wait for me to give her any grandchildren, which is what she was obviously hinting at," he said with a tut and then a smile.

"So, Jack, when are you going to tell them about, well, you know?"

Jack gave a huge sigh as he knew Mandy was right and he couldn't avoid it for much longer.

"Soon, it'll have to be soon. They're my parents and they should know, and they deserve to know the truth about me. Just like you deserved to know. Especially when you said earlier about you and the boss.'

"I knew that I had to tell you because I couldn't go on behind your back. Him, or just about anyone else, wouldn't have bothered me, but not you, even if it risked damaging our friendship. Because after my parents and other members of my family, you are the most important person in my life and have been for many years. Even if you do drive me mad sometimes, I wouldn't change you for the world," he said, taking hold of her hand as they both ensured that their fingers interlocked tightly.

"How do you think they will take it?" she asked . "Well, that's the million-dollar question, isn`t it? Shocked at first, I guess. That's only to be expected really, what with me being the only child, and there's more chance of them seeing Lord Lucan swimming alongside the Loch Ness Monster than me giving them a grandchild anytime soon. But I reckon that once they get over the initial shock, they'll accept it, and once they do, and only when they do, that's when I'll start telling other people, but I'll tell you one thing for certain, Mandy."

"What's that?"

"There's no way that I'm telling the rugby team," he said, which he was extremely adamant about.

"Why not?" asked Mandy, not really understanding why he was so against telling them.

"No bloody way! Have you seen the size of our front row?" asked Jack.

"No."

"Well, if you ever do, you'll know why I'm not exactly keen on the idea of telling them anything. Anyway, I was planning on giving up the game," he said, as Mandy immediately looked disappointed on hearing this.

"What for?" she began. "Is it because of this front row you just said about, because if it is, you just let me talk to them, alright, and by the time that I'm done with them, they wouldn't even dare to think about touching you, okay. You shouldn't be scared to say anything, Jack. I mean, it's 1998 now, not the Dark Ages, times have changed, people have changed, and are more willing to accept each other these days. So go, just tell them, Jack, you may just be pleasantly surprised by the outcome."

"Maybe you're right, Mandy," he said after a moments serious consideration.

"Will you really, Jack? Oh I'm so pleased," Mandy said, genuinely happy to hear what he had just said. "Yeah, I'll leave them a letter after I've left," Jack said with a grin.

"Walked into that one, didn't I?"

"Yes, you did. Look, Mandy, it's not that I don`t appreciate what you're saying or anything, because I do, I really do, but I was seriously thinking about giving up the game.

Truthfully, I was. I just don't really enjoy it anymore and, to be honest, I haven't done for quite some time. And I was never really that good at it. I only kept going for the drinking sessions afterwards. Or maybe, I was trying to be someone that I'm clearly not," he said, with no real regret about it.

"Well, if you're sure, Jack," she said, trying to be as understanding as possible.

"Yes, I'm sure. Bugger `em. Not in that sense, you understand, if you'll excuse the slip of the tongue."

"You're excused," Mandy said, as they both saw the funny side of Jack's last comment.

He took a breath and asked, "What about you then, Mandy, about the baby I mean? Are you going to keep it? Are you going to tell the boss?"

"Yeah, I'm keeping the baby. I decided that the very moment the doctor confirmed it, there was no doubt in my mind about that, but as for the boss, I'm not telling him anything. Not a single word. Especially after all he's done, having all those affairs with at least four other girls, and that's just we know about, could be loads of others that we don't.

"He doesn't deserve to be a father, especially not to my child, because let's face it, he's not exactly the greatest role model around now, is he?" she said, meaning every word.

"When you put it like that, you're right, no doubt about that, but on the other hand though, he should be made to give you at least half of his fortune for you and the baby. But I suppose the dangerous side to that is, if you expect him to pay up, he's going to probably expect visiting rights as the father and all that," he said.

But Mandy was having none of that.

"He can claim all the rights that that he wants. There's not a chance in hell that he'll be seeing my baby. Not in a million years."

"Again, totally get it, but isn't it worth it, letting him see the baby, even if it's only once a fortnight or something, so that you can rightfully get your hands on his fortune so that the baby doesn't go without?" he puts to her, but again, Mandy puts her foot firmly down.

"I mean it, Jack, there's no way that he's going to spend any time with my baby as I'm not even going to tell him anything, but I take the point you made about the money and don't worry, I'll make him pay for what he's done, just you wait and see. I'll think of something."

PART NINE

The Plan

Jack was all for extorting any sort of money out of the boss, and so decided to try and think of some sort of a plan himself that would help him, and Mandy do just that, and if in the process he could add an element of embarrassment for the boss as well, then that would be a nice bonus. But no matter how hard he tried, nothing would come to mind, much to his ever-growing frustration. But thankfully for him, he then saw a huge and mischievous grin on Mandy's face.

"What are you grinning for?" he asked.

"Oh, nothing."

"That grin on your face right now does not suggest nothing. Quite the opposite in fact, so come on, spill," he said.

"Just thought of something," she told him. "Oh yeah, like what?"

"How we can exact some sort of revenge on the boss," Mandy said, with more than a naughty glint in her eye, which matched her grin nicely.

"Well, don't keep it yourself," Jack said, dying to know what she had thought of.

"Alright then," she began. "Ask yourself this, where's the best place that we can hurt him?"

Jack immediately thought he knew the answer to this. "A good hard kick between his legs."

"What? He liked it rough as well, did he? He never told me that. If I'd known that, I could have given him a smack in the mouth every time we were in the bedroom together and putting on the bondage gear, or maybe during the session, because like I said earlier, I'm always up for a bit of experimenting."

Jack looked at her, totally baffled.

"What? What? No, no, not in that sense. I mean, a proper real good, hard kick between the legs. Right in the crown jewels. Especially when he's not expecting it."

Mandy suddenly got it. "Oh sorry, I'm with you now, sorry."

"How can you even be thinking of about anything sexual at a time like this?" Jack just had to ask.

"Oh, it's just when you said about kicking between the legs, I just thought how some people like that sort of thing, you know, rough and all that," she said, as Jack couldn't really argue with her on that one, before she continues. "Even though it's not such a bad idea, especially if I were wearing stilettos at the time, and I could drive the pointed end right in there, but I was thinking of somewhere else that would be just as painful and could easily bring more than a few tears to his eyes."

"Oh really, like where?" an intrigued Jack asked.

"His wallet."

"Hang on a second, you just sat there less than two minutes ago and said that you wanted nothing to do with the boss," he said.

"Woman's prerogative. Anyway, what I'm thinking about is not just money for child maintenance and the occasional holiday along with decent presents at Christmas."

"No, what I'm thinking about is proper money. Money that not only can set us up but can also make a real dent into his bank account."

"Oh, okay then, with you now. So, what's your plan?" Jack asked.

"Quite simple really, just go around to the factory one night when everyone has gone home and rob   him of all the spare cash that he has there," she said, which was not the answer that he was expecting.

"Oh, so not just simply tell his wife everything, and in case you're wondering, I'd be happy to tell her about me as well, in the hope that she'll then divorce him and take him to the cleaners," Jack said, to which Mandy did give some consideration to.

"Yeah, could do that as well if you want. A detailed letter perhaps, yeah, with times, dates, and places. That's good thinking, Jack. But listen to this. He keeps thousands, and I really mean literally thousands, in that safe he has in his office, which he hides not only from his wife but from the taxman as well, which he often bragged to me was as safe as houses because of the brand-new security system that he had installed."

"How do you know all of this?" a very curious Jack asked.

"He showed me it all during one of our Wednesdays together. He thought it might be exciting to do it at the factory for a change to act out a fantasy of his."

Jack's ears instantly pricked up on hearing this. "Oh really? A fantasy, eh, and an outdoor one at that.

Thought that you only liked to do your experimenting in the confounds of the bedroom alone," Jack said.

"Normally, you'd be right in saying that Jack, but he was having some difficulties with some of the bondage gear, and between me and you, it was taking a little of the fun out of it. Every Wednesday, week in and week out, always having to help him with, at times, some of the basic stuff likes handcuffs and the odd chain. So, when he suggested to me about maybe being interested in another form of experimentation that would take place in the privacy of his own office, I thought why not, variety is the spice of life and all that," Mandy told him.

"Oh right, okay, so what was this fantasy then? I'm dying to know," said Jack, and Mandy duly obliged.

PART TEN

The Safe

"Well, it went a bit like this. We were supposed to burglars. Well, when I say burglars, more like fugitives from justice, on the run, and we're looking for somewhere safe to hide out for the night, and if we could find somewhere with a safe that we could crack, then all the better, before we complete our getaway and make our way abroad.

"All seemed to be going okay, that was until we heard the local Chief Constable through a megaphone telling us to give ourselves up as he had the place surrounded. We were going to hold out for as long as possible before we thought about making a Butch and Sundance style break for freedom, but before we do, we decide that we have one final, well, you know, but before we did, he showed me everything, the lot."

"All the secret combinations that were needed to shut off the main door alarm before entering the building, and once inside, showing me how to turn off the CCTV, which I insisted on beforehand because there was no way I was going to run the risk of there being mucky films of me going around.

"And honestly, Jack, when he opened his safe to put some money into it, I thought my eyes were going to pop out of my head. I'd never seen so much cash in one place, ever. And when I asked him how much was actually there, he had no problem telling me that he has never anything less than one-hundred thousand in there at any one time. Just like he had no problem telling me the combination to the safe."

"And he really trusted you with that?" asked Jack. "Yeah."

"What a bloody fool."

"Yes, he was. Must have been thinking that I was still the poor, little factory girl who he managed to con into bed to begin with, but how wrong he was. Trust me, Jack, this'll be like taking candy from a baby, and after, we can move away from here, have a fresh start somewhere else, because I don't even want to be in the same town as him anymore."

"Even if it was just for his own sanity, Jack had to take a moment to take in what she had just said to him. "Okay, stop right there for a moment, Mandy... Are you mental? Firstly, what's this 'we' business?" he asked.

"Well, he did do the dirty on you as well. Just thought you'd like to get some of your own back also."

Jack did see the logic of what she just said.

"Okay, let's just say that if, and I mean it's a big if, I do agree to this, where exactly are you thinking that we move to?"

"Funny you should say that Jack, because I've just this very second thought of the perfect place where we could go," she said, smiling.

"Had a funny feeling that you were going to say something like that," Jack began, and braced himself for the worse. "So, go on then, where's that?" he asked.

Mandy had no hesitation in telling him. "Spain." "You what? Spain!" Jack cried out, not being able to hide his shock on hearing this.

Mandy remained utterly calm and simply said, "Yeah."

"Spain? As in across the Channel and next to France, but nowhere near Estonia?" Jack said just as calmly as before.

Mandy answered, "Yeah. Well, I think so anyway." "You know something," Jack began with a very concerned look clearly across his face, "I've got this very strange feeling that you're really serious about all of this, and I can't deny, it's scaring me a little bit." "Of course, I'm serious. Why shouldn't we get our own back on the boss after all that he's done to us? And trust me, Jack, this'll be easy," she said, with a frightening air of confidence, which made Jack feel even more uneasy.

"Easy for you maybe," he said, which left Mandy slightly bemused.

"What do you mean, easy for me?" she asked. "Because I'm not like you," he pointed out.

"Well, obviously, I mean, you're a man, and I'm a woman," she pointed out in return.

"No, not like that," Jack said.

"Well, what then?" Mandy asked, not really understanding what he meant.

"Look, don't take this the wrong way, because I'm not having a go at you, but I've never committed a crime in my life. I wouldn't know where to start or even if I have the guts to actually go through with it, whereas you, well, I'm not saying that you're some hardened criminal type that needs locking away for life or anything like that, but I also think it's fair to say that you're not exactly new to criminal activity either," which was something that Mandy was happy to admit to.

"Point and no offence taken," she began by saying. "But honestly, Jack, don't worry about a thing. You can just keep lookout, okay, if it makes you feel better. C`mon, what do you say?"

"I don't know, Mandy, it still seems very dodgy to me," Jack told her, still not really convinced that her plan was as easy as she was making it out to be.

"Look, Jack, trust me, I've got it all covered. We'll just go around there in the van and, like I said, you can wait outside and keep watch, and I'll be in and out before you know it, with a massive bundle of cash, and then we can start a new life away from here and, most importantly, away from the boss," she said with her eyes literally pleading with him to say yes, but Jack still had his doubts about all of this.

"I still don't know, Mandy, it still sounds all very risky to me," he said somewhat nervously, as Mandy moved her chair closer to him and put a reassuring arm around him.

"Please, Jack, trust me on this one, I won't let you down, I promise," she said, and it's not that he didn't want to trust her or anything like that, but this is still the girl who was convinced that a perfume called Long Poo would make her a nice, tidy profit.

"So, you say that his safe is always brimming over with cash?" he asked.

"Literally rammed with it," she said.

"And he told you nothing less than one-hundred thousand?" he asked, becoming ever more intrigued by the minute.

"And that's on a bad day. Could easily be more than that by the time that we get there, Jack," she said, as he looked at her, seeing nothing but the truth coming from her eyes. Because if there was a single word of untruth in what she had just said, then he would have spotted it easily, as she was known to blink rather rapidly when she was telling lies in the past. And she hadn't blinked once. But he still had questions for her.

"But why abroad? Or more to the point, why Spain?"

"Because I need to, Jack. I've done nothing but make a right mess of my life and I need to change all of that, and I honestly believe that I cannot do it here. I need a new environment, not just for me, but for my baby as well. Plus, if the boss ever finds out about the baby, he'll never leave me alone. Even if we move as far north as Scotland. He often said to me how he always wanted to be a father, but his wife was never really all that keen on the idea, so if he ever finds out about me, trust me, Jack, he'll hire the best private investigators if necessary.

"Because if he wants something badly enough, sooner or later, he usually gets it. Suppose that's why he's been so successful in business.

"That's why abroad, Jack, because I feel that's the best chance I've got of disappearing, so that I can be totally free of him and, at the same time, give myself a chance to build a new life for myself and the baby."

Jack looked kindly at her as he knew exactly what she meant by it all.

"Okay, I get it, as I know just as much or even better than a lot of people that life at times hasn't exactly dealt you a good hand, so I can understand perfectly why you would want to do this."

"Thanks Jack, I knew that you'd understand. So, when we do this, if we take the van with all those jeans in and park just outside the front entrance and then leave it there, because even though he'll be no doubt very upset when he realised that his secret stash has gone, he'll get even more angry when he sees the police turnup, after receiving a call from a law-abiding citizen, and start asking him questions about those smuggled jeans, which just happen to be in a van that's registered to him and is parked very conveniently outside his factory," she said, very much liking the sound of her own idea.

"You really have thought about this, haven't you?" said Jack.

"Told you that I had, Jack, so please trust me on this one alright because it's going to be just like I said, taking candy from a baby."

PART ELEVEN

The Promise

"Yeah, I know you said, and being honest, now that I've thought about it myself a little, it does sound good. Not just robbing the boss, but I've always fancied the idea of having an all-year-round tan without having to pay a fortune in a solarium for it…

…" parents will be shocked as anything when I tell them that I'm moving abroad…

"Christ, imagine their faces when I tell them that I am gay as well… Double shocker. Mum will probably stay away from the local Conservative Club for quite a while when I tell her that one.

"But just like Dad, she'll be okay and get over it all… eventually," said Jack, as he looked at Mandy, who was ready to burst out with joy and excitement.

She then asked, just to be certain, "Does that mean you'll do it then?"

He gave quite a stern and serious look, before telling her, "There are conditions."

Mandy knew that he meant this. "Okay, like what, Jack?"

"Firstly, no more of these stupid, dodgy, money-making deals that you keep getting yourself involved in. "You never were any good at them, and if we're going to be living abroad, we're going to need every penny that we can get our hands on and not rely on what's in the boss's safe." Mandy knew he was right.

"Okay, Jack, whatever you say. But I only started doing them in the hope that I could make some extra money to give to you. To say thanks for everything that you`ve done for me over the years," she said with genuine sincerity, which Jack did appreciate. "How many times have I told you? There's never been any need to thank me, alright. Wish you'd get that through your thick skull.

"And secondly, no more fighting, and that especially applies to hitting policemen. You're pregnant, remember?" Jack told her.

"Okay, I know, I know. But he did start it, Jack. He was stood by the main entrance of the building looking like he was waiting for me and just started mouthing off, calling me all sorts of names.

"I tried ignoring him, but he just kept on and on until he dared me to hit him. So, I did. About four, five, maybe even six or seven times. Truth was, it wasn't much of a fight really. After I'd finished hitting him, he just went down like a sack of spuds.

"Completely forget that I might have been pregnant at the time, that's how much he wound me up. I was on my way to the doctor's when this happened.

"But I promise you, Jack, from now on, no more trouble," she said, crossing her heart, as Jack looks very closely at her and he had no doubt that she had every intention of keeping her word, but then again, this is Mandy.

"Okay, so when do you want to do this madness then?" he said.

"Well, it'll have to be soon, 'cause gonorrhea could be back at any time with not only the rest of the STD Squad, but also with a bundle full of warrants, and knowing my luck, there'll be a new Chief Constable and the photos will be useless," she said.

"Oh yeah, forgot about them. Right, it's Thursday today, so, if we go and see your parents tomorrow, then see mine on Saturday, as it's going to take a lot longer for me to explain things to them. No offence."

"Again, none taken."

"Good to hear. Then, after, we'll contact the landlord now that we're giving up this place. What do you think? Let him keep the furniture so he can sell it and keep the money for himself?" Mandy just nodded in agreement.

"Alright then, and we'll hit the factory Sunday night, then after, it's straight to the airport," said Jack. "Are you sure that you want to, Jack? You honestly and truly want to do this?" Mandy just had to ask. "Yes, yes, I mean it, Mandy. Let's do it, shall we, because we both know that you couldn't survive by yourself. You'd probably be in prison within a month."

Mandy had never felt such joy and excitement in her entire life as she began literally jumping around the kitchen.

"Yes, yes, yes!" she began to cry out through her smiles and laughter, and it wasn`t that he didn`t want to see his dearest friend so happy, because nothing gave him greater pleasure, but Jack did have to remind her of something.

"Alright, alright, I get it, you're happy and excited and that's great, but please calm yourself down, you've got a baby inside of you, remember?" he said, and it didn't appear that she heard him at first, but her bouncing around came to an abrupt halt. Although, the smile and the energy that she was now feeling could have not only powered their flat, but the entire building for at least a month, as she eventually caught her breath.

PART TWELVE

The End

"Oh my God, yes! Oh, Jack, you won't regret this, I promise. I've got it all worked out. My Uncle Frank moved out there a few years ago after he had that Lottery win, and he always said that it was the best thing that he'd ever done. He's often said that I could go out there and live with him anytime I want, and I know that he wouldn't mind if you came along.

"You'll like him a lot, he's a top bloke, and I've no doubt that you two will hit it off. I'll send him an email just before we go to let him know that we're on our way. He'll look after us, Jack, you'll see. Oh Jack, just think about it, a whole new life together, just us two, and the baby, of course," she said, giving him a huge hug before she sits down again.

"I know, it's mad, isn't it?" he said.

"Mad? It's not mad. Okay, maybe a little bit it is, but it'll also be perfect as well. Me, you, and when the baby comes along, we could be sort of like a little family together.

"Finding work won't be a problem either because with his winnings, Uncle Frank bought himself a little pub and restaurant type of place, and I'm sure that he wouldn't say no to another couple of helping hands."

"That's alright then, be good to have a steady wage," Jack began, before pausing for thought momentarily. "Strange, isn`t it? I've never even thought of emigrating before, not once in my entire life, but here I am, just about to jet off to Spain on what could easily be seen as a whim."

"Oh, and not forgetting, the small matter of helping you commit a robbery. Never stolen so much as a penny sweet in my life, so this'll be another first for me as well. Let's be honest, Mandy, life certainly isn't dull with you around, eh?"

"Well, when you put it like that, Jack, I suppose it isn't, but I reckon I need some dull and boring in my life right now. Got a baby to think of, haven't I? That's why I need you in my life, Jack, need you to keep me on the straight and narrow, no matter which country we're in; I can't do it by myself," she told him, making sure that she took hold of his hand again, which seemed to demonstrate the special bond that clearly existed between them.

Just like Jack's mother had always said, as he looks back at her, silently promising that he'd always be there for her whenever she needed him, but he still had something else that he felt he had to discuss with her.

"Right, Mandy, I do need to talk to you about something that I think is very important and I'd rather sort this out now before anything else happens, okay."

"Yeah, okay, Jack, I'm all ears."

"Right, look, this plan of yours is massive, and there could very well be certain implications involved sometime in the future," he said.

"Implications? How do you mean, Jack?"

"What I mean is, Mandy, is quite simply, you are a gorgeous and very sexy-looking girl, and I know for a fact that there have been plenty of lads around here who have fancied you for ages."

"And out in Spain, under all that sunshine, all those well-tanned lads with their ripped muscle bodies out there walking around in just their tight vests and even tighter shorts, well, there could easily come a time when you may just want to be with a man again.

"If you catch my drift? And being totally honest about this, possibly just like me as well, especially if they do look like what I've just described, wanting to be with a man that is."

"But not the same one this time," they both suddenly said in unison, which they both saw the funny side to.

Mandy then said, "I hear you, Jack, totally get where you are coming from, I really do. But being totally honest with you now, what the boss has done to both of us, it's put me off men possibly for life. But, if I do get any urges that a freezing cold shower won't cure, then look, we're both adults, Jack, I'm sure that we can work something out, alright. Just remember that the most important thing, and I mean this on my baby's life, is that you're the best thing that's ever happened to me, Jack, and you are absolutely right when you said that I'd be in prison within a month without you.

"Truth is, I'd be surprised if I lasted a month. I truly think the world of you, Jack, always have done and I always will, and I promise that I'll never ever leave you."

Knowing that she had spoken straight from her heart, Jack felt reassured enough to say, "And I promise I`ll never leave you either."

"Right, so that's all sorted out then," said Mandy.

"Yes, all sorted. Right, suppose I'd better start packing. Oh, is your passport still valid?" he asked. "Yes."

"Good, because the last thing that we want to happen is to do all this and then get to the airport and find that we can't even get to Spain, or anywhere else abroad for that matter," he said, relieved.

"Well, you can stop worrying about that, Jack, it's all sorted."

"Good to hear," said Jack, as he got up and started to make his way out of the kitchen, but before he finally leaves, "Mandy?"

"Yeah."

"Just one more thing before I start packing." "What's that then, Jack?"

"There were these three men in a pub one night…"

"Hold it right there, Jack, why don't you save it for on the plane, alright. I want to write an important letter now and I don't want to forget any details due to laughing, okay."

Jack thought hard about what she had just said. "Yes, you're right, you could lose concentration. See you in a while," he said as he left the kitchen and disappeared into his bedroom.

On hearing his bedroom door close, Mandy stood up and went over to the kitchen drawer, which is next to the sink, and took out a notepad and pen, sitting back down. She was itching to write but as she began to recollect all the nights that they spent together, which, to begin with, did bring a smile to her face as she couldn't deny to herself that it wasn't all bad. Especially when she had driven around in the Rolls Royce.

But the smile was very soon to disappear as she couldn't forget or even forgive him for what he had done not only to her but to Jack as well, as she just threw the pen down on the table and picked up her mobile and dialled.

"Oh, hello there, how are you?"

"It's Mandy."

"Mandy, you know, the one that works for you."

"Every Wednesday night."

"Yes, that Mandy."

"Oh, no reason, just called to see how you are, and who's that woman I can hear the background because I'm certain that's not your wife's voice."

"Let me think now, it's Thursday, so it must be Sandra."

"You what? Well, a woman just knows these things."

"What's that?"

"She means nothing to you and I'm still the one that you want to be with?"

"Aww, well that's nice to hear. Even though I don't think she liked the sound of that judging by what I can hear her saying to you now."

"Not very ladylike, is it? Then again, she was never known for being one in the first place."

"Oh, like I said, no real reason, just to see how you are, and while I've got you on the phone, there's something that I'd like to share with you, which I think you just might like."

"Well, there were these three men in a pub one night, and all three were eyeing up the barmaid, you see, and then the first man said, 'Do you know that I bought that barmaid a gin and tonic and a packet of crisps, then she let me sleep with her.'

The second man then said, 'Well, I bought her a brandy and a sausage roll, then she let me sleep with her.' So, the third man then said, 'Well, that barmaid is my wife, so I don't have to buy her anything to get her to sleep with me.'"

"You liked that one, did you?"

"Thought you might."

"Anyway, just called to see how you are."

"Yes, I gather that you're busy now."

"You what, see me next Wednesday as usual? You might."

"Tell, you what, if you're a good boy and you can squeeze me into your busy schedule, I may even arrange a little treat for you before then."

"You'll just have to wait and see now, won't you?"

"Have I ever disappointed you before, huh?"

"Think we both know that I haven't."

"Right, well, you'll just have to organise something then, won't you?"

"Okay, I'll wait for your call then, shall I, tiger? Alright, see you soon, bye."

Mandy then hangs up and throws her phone angrily down on the table, lucky that she didn't damage it in the process, once again feeling the pain of a scorned woman.

She then said through a snarl, "Not if I see you first, pal!"

As she picked up the pen and began writing feverishly, she not only knew what to write, but exactly who to write to.